I0518217

MISTLETOE MELTDOWN

BEST SELLING AUTHOR
RACHEL RAWLINGS

All rights reserved. No part of this publication may be reproduced, distributed, or transmitted in any form or by any means, including photocopying, recording, or other electronic or mechanical methods, without the prior written permission of the publisher, except in the case of brief quotations embodied in critical reviews and certain other non-commercial uses permitted by copyright law.

Mistletoe Meltdown
A Maurin Kincaide Short Story
Rachel Rawlings

ISBN: 0692542124
ISBN-13: 978-0692542125

Copyright © 2015 Rachel Rawlings
www.RachelRawlings.com

Published in the United States by: R Squared Publishing
www.Hallowread.com

This is a work of fiction. Names, characters, businesses, places, events and incidents are either the products of the author's imagination or used in a fictitious manner. Any resemblance to actual persons, living or dead, or actual events is purely coincidental.

Cover and formatting by Incredibook Design

DEDICATION

Dear Santa,

I'm sure you checked your list not once but twice, came to realize I'm a lot more naughty than nice. But the bad guys deserve it. I promise it's true, so how about giving me a new glock or two?

Xoxo Maurin

Books By Rachel Rawlings

The Maurin Kincaide Series
The Morrigna
Witch Hunt
Wolfsbane
Blood Bath
Ill Fated

Coming Soon
Payable On Death, a Jax Rhoades novel
A Haunted Life
It's All Death To Me

MISTLETOE MELTDOWN

"Chestnuts roasting on an open fire, Jack Frost nipping at your nose. Yuletide carols being sung by a choir and folks dressed up like Eskimos." Nat King Cole's smooth voice blared from the outdoor speakers hidden in the greenery that turned the walking mall into a winter wonderland, soothing the savage holiday shopping beasts surrounding me. I tried not to overanalyze the lyrics but I'd met the Hoar Frost King once and he'd do a lot more than nip at your nose.

Besides, did anyone really have a Christmas like the ones people sang about?

The Kincaide's, my adoptive family, practiced every holiday tradition from Midnight Mass to the extravagant family dinner to a house staged similar to something from a *Martha Stewart Living* magazine. It didn't change anything. The tinsel and twinkling lights only highlighted the hatred.

So imagine my enthusiasm when my real father Arawn suggested we have a Christmas/Solstice dinner. With friends. At my apartment. I understood his need to create memories--he'd missed out on most of my life--but as a self-proclaimed Scrooge I'd avoided anything to do with the holidays since I'd left Beacon Hill at seventeen. But here I was layered up underneath my leather jacket, knit hat pulled down to my eyebrows, basically dressed like the aforementioned Eskimo.

The numbness in my hands increased with each block I walked back to my car. Not from the cold--my purple wool gloves did a decent job--but from the shopping bags cutting of my circulation. I loaded up the Rabriolet, an old metallic blue VW so named because the guy who sold it took all the Rabbit badges off and replaced them with Cabriolet, the convertible's small trunk barely holding my haul of gifts and groceries for tonight's festivities.

The temperature inside the car barely rose a degree

above the outside temperature during the short drive back to my apartment. I pulled into the parking space I'd shoveled out this morning after the snow stopped but didn't rush to get out of the car. Two pep talks later I dragged myself and my multitude of bags up the three flights of stairs which led to my place.

In a few hours every seat in the house would be filled. All of my friends and new family were invited, something else my father insisted upon. The list wasn't long--my apartment is just that small. Four fae including Conry, three vampires, two wolves, one witch--and a partridge in a pear tree. I set the groceries on the kitchen counter and dropped the rest of the bags by the tree I'd yet to decorate.

Mason - the boyfriend – had had a beautiful Nordmann fir delivered this morning. Its symmetrical branches created the perfect pyramid of lush foliage. Mrs. Kincaide would have been green with envy, a shade deep enough to rival the dark color of the needles. The tree's heavy aroma, combined with the cinnamon scented pine cones in a bowl on the coffee table, made the entire apartment smell like a traditional Christmas but I'd chosen a winter wonderland theme for the decorations to represent the Solstice. Glittering white snowflakes and icicles spilled out of boxes, waiting to be hung. Three strands of new led lights lay next to the crystal snowflake I'd chosen instead of the usual angel or star.

Overwhelmed barely began to describe how I felt when I looked at all the things still undone.

I decided to prep the food and save the tree for last. Far from domesticated, I fumbled my way through the only recipe for a main course I thought I could manage, root vegetables, sliced and diced with pot roast. I opened a bottle of Menage a Trois, letting the red wine breathe before I poured the first glass. Several more bottles of wine and liquor lined the counter.

Once the oven preheated I slid the roast in and focused my attention on dessert. In other words I took the pastries I purchased from the bakery beneath Mason's apartment in town and arranged them on a platter. With a wine glass in one hand and a bottle in the other I went back to the tree, stringing the lights and hanging each ornament carefully. Conry stayed on the couch, watching me walk circles around the tree as I pondered the age old question - to tinsel or not to tinsel? Satisfied with the way everything looked I opted against it.

Three different offers to help get everything ready and I turned down everyone. I needed the time alone, cooking and decorating, to mentally prepare myself.

Ten yuletides had come and gone since the last time I took part in any festivities. A farewell if you will. I walked out of Castle Kincaide on New Year's Eve. The symbolism was lost on everyone but me. This time of year meant something entirely different to me. It wasn't a religious experience. For me it was a rebirth. Like a phoenix, I left my old life in ashes and rose up from the smoldering embers as something new--my own person. After giving it some thought, I realized what the season meant to me was remarkably similar to my father's Solstice—a celebration of the life, death and rebirth of deities.

With less than an hour to spare before everyone arrived, it was time to wrap presents. I voted against the idea of giving gifts, having recalled the time I saved my lunch money to buy something for my little sister Frankie and my parents at the holiday bazaar at school. Saying it didn't go well would be an understatement. After that, I'd pretty much sworn off gift giving.

However, I'd been outvoted.

Now I sat before a pile of boxes, tissue paper, scotch tape, wrapping paper and bows. At the greeting card store I'd started with an armful of gift bags because I didn't think my duct tape gift wrap idea would be appreciated but as I approached the register I noticed all the different types of wrapping paper. Dazzled by the array of patterns and colors, I'd come to a conclusion. Gift bags were a cop-out. If I had to do it, it wouldn't be half ass. I'd selected nine rolls of paper, one for each gift, something that represented the recipient.

For Arawn, silver paper embossed with a winter scene of stags and trees which for some reason reminded me of my first encounter with him. The dark green paper with silver stags and evergreens I picked for Mason was perfect for the hunter in the family and similar enough to my father's to acknowledge both as members of the Wild Hunt. Camo for Cash, a nod to his special ops days and the way we first met. My pick for Nolak didn't come from the Christmas paper but the midnight blue with silver wolves still seemed appropriate. I chose white paper with glittering snowflakes for Amalie, the sparkles reminding me of her personality.

Aidan and Ryanne had similar plaids in rich shades

of burgundy and green, a nod to the new clan they were forming together. For Dre it wasn't so much the green paper as the beautiful cream colored french ribbon. And for my beloved Conry I selected the biggest red bow I could find. With my decision to personalize each package came the first stirrings of holiday spirit. Each gift wrapped and placed under the tree stirred up a little bit more.

By the time everyone began to arrive I'd finished the first bottle of wine and felt down right merry. Amalie brought a beautiful tray of cheeses, fruit and nuts. Aidan brought a case of bottled blood for himself, Ryanne and Dre. Cash and Nolak carried in an alarming amount of holiday music and movies.

Mason brought a bough of mistletoe, holding it above our heads as he crossed the threshold. That was a holiday tradition I could get behind. I stepped into him, softly kissing the lips I'd been missing all day. His other arm wrapped around me, pressing our bodies together as he deepened the kiss and silently promised more. Satisfied with my weakened knees and rapid heart he walked me into the living room before making a beeline to the tree, where he hung a beautiful ice blue glass letter M ornament. It stood out from all the others, because I knew it was more than my first initial. It was his as well, a symbol of us. I felt the ice around my heart melt a little bit more.

All these emotions called for more wine.

My father arrived, arms full of packages and party trays with a contagious smile on his face. When I returned his smile with one of my own, his comment on how much I looked like my mother had me scurrying off to check on the roast. I blamed the lingering teary eyes on the blast of hot air which escaped when I opened the oven. With no pending disaster or threat of death the evening already felt a lot like one of those Christmas songs I heard earlier in the day.

Cash gathered us all in the living room for one of his family's favorite traditions. After taking a few jabs about it being too cold outside to play fetch he turned on *A Christmas Story* while the rest of us ruined our dinner with more drinks and appetizers. While the credits rolled he told us about Christmas morning as a kid, they'd open presents, stay in their pajamas and watch the all-day marathon of the movie until it was time for dinner.

His comment reminded me to check on the roast. I waved off the offers of help in the kitchen, preferring to listen to all of them swap stories of varied holiday celebrations and traditions, something I'd never experienced growing up despite appearances.

I served the best dinner I'd ever cooked. The only real dinner I'd ever cooked actually. There were no awkward and uncomfortable silences during the meal. Not even between Ryanne and I. My father convinced me to invite her with a speech about how things worked out for the best and a new slight wouldn't repair old wounds. The conversation flowed and I fed Conry under the table while my father regaled us with tales of the great Solstice feasts in the days when only one court ruled the Fae. Most of my roast beef made it into Conry's mouth before my father stopped mid-sentence to point out he knew what I was doing and remind me that Cwnn Anfwnn did not eat table scraps. With a wink in my direction he went back to his story and I finished my potatoes and carrots.

By the time his story ended every plate was cleared. Not a drop of blood or morsel of food remained. Glasses were raised and toasts were made, for the hostess, for the meal and for the witch who obviously spelled my kitchen to produce delicious food regardless of who cooked it. I'd seen and done some weird stuff in my life. A holiday party with vampires, werewolves, fae and a witch should be on that list but it wasn't. It was as close to perfection as I'd experienced.

Like the proverbial kid on Christmas, Amalie ushered everyone back into the living room to open the bar and our gifts before dessert. I whole-heartedly supported her plan because there was no way I could eat another bite. With a vodka and cranberry juice in hand I settled on the couch with Mason and Conry. Amalie took on the roll of Santa, passing out gifts to everyone. I watched as the beautiful paper and bows piled up, the carnage of Christmas spread across my carpet.

My anxiety built as I waited for my gifts to be opened. Why were mine handed out last? Why was this such a big deal? If they didn't like what I picked out I had gift receipts, they could just exchange it for something else.

So why did it feel like they'd be rejecting me instead?

Conry, always in tune with my emotional state, picked up on my unrest and nestled in closer as a sign of support. Mason threw an arm over my shoulder and pulled me against his chest, whispering in my ear. "Take a deep breath. Relax. They're gifts, not grenades."

"I think I'd handle it better if they were. It's just...

Forget it. I'm great, everything is great." I looked up at him with my best smile in place knowing full well he wasn't fooled.

Mason gave my hand a little squeeze as Dre opened his gift, whispering reassurances he would love whatever was inside. I remained skeptical until the hand carved pipe and tobacco came out of the box and Dre lit up. I considered letting him smoke in my apartment after seeing his smile when I told him the clerk at the cigar shop said the tobacco smelled like sugar cookies. He assured me he could wait to go outside until after everyone opened their gifts.

Amalie picked up a box, grinning when she realized it was from me. The sparkly paper matched the excitement in her eyes, just like I'd thought it would. She carefully slit the taped seams so the heavy paper didn't tear and pulled it back from the box. "We used to make book covers out of pretty paper like this when I was a kid. I've got a journal at home this would be perfect for." She lifted the lid on the box, gasping when she saw the grimmoire inside. "Are you serious? This is freaking amazing! It's way better than the Swavorski crystal skull earrings I got you."

"I guess this is my clue to open your gift." I reached

in the gift bag and pulled out the green tissue paper to reach the jewelry inside. The earrings were beautiful and obviously custom-made, eight tiny silver interlocking loops creating a chain effect and held a black crystal skull. Mason swept my hair back, holding it in a makeshift ponytail so I could hook them in. I didn't wear a lot of jewelry. In my line of work, earrings could cost you an earlobe but these were surprisingly light weight and went perfectly with just about everything I owned, so I could definitely wear them on my off time.

Tired of waiting, Conry sniffed around the tree until he found the giant bone and collar I got him. Not interested in the collar, he left it under the tree and dragged the rawhide off to the corner. The sound of crunching and gnawing drowned out Danny Elfman's song *Making Christmas* playing on one of Cash's cds.

Aidan wrapped himself up in the charcoal cashmere scarf and donned the silk and cashmere grey herringbone ivy cap, impressed I'd remembered his measurements. I'd put the least amount of thought into Ryanne's green scarf but she seemed to like it. The wolf sculpture I bought for Nolak and the small oil painting of an alpha and his pack in the moonlight I found for Cash were a big hit. You'd be more likely to find weapons than art at either of their places but I could tell they appreciated the likeness to their wolves.

Surrounded by books, band shirts and chocolate covered espresso beans, I'd already given and received some pretty awesome gifts. But the two presents yet to be opened were the ones I was the most excited about. I watched nervously as my father finally picked my gift, taking his time and examining the pattern on the paper. He finally unwrapped it and opened the box, pulling out the pocket watch.

"So you can keep track of time here when you're in Other World." I blurted out the reasoning behind the gift before I could catch myself, cursing under my breath. I sounded way too desperate for approval and I knew it.

He pressed the button on the top of the watch. With a soft click it popped open, exposing the inside cover. His thumb traced the edge of the gold circle before resting on the black and white picture of me inside. "If only it kept track of you." He leaned forward, pressing a kiss to my forehead. "I have been given two priceless treasures in my life. This is one. The other is you."

As if by magic, and maybe it was knowing my

father, he held open his hand. A small portrait in a simple oval shaped wooden frame sat center of his palm. "It is the only picture I have of her and now it belongs to you. She swore allowing someone to capture her image also meant they could capture a piece of your soul. She gave the artist less than an hour to paint her likeness. I have our life together, all of the memories. Every time I close my eyes she dances on the edge of my vision. You should have something of her."

I managed not to cry. Barely. I considered myself a hard ass but damn it all if my father didn't have me on the verge of tears twice in one night. "I don't know what to say. Thank you."

"I'm next." Mason shifted on the couch, preparing to give me my present when my phone started going off. "Seriously? You have got to be kidding me." Mason muttered under his breath along with a few other choice words about what he planned to do to whoever was on the other end of the line. His voice was low enough I barely heard him so I was pretty sure no one else did but it definitely had me wondering what exactly my Solstice gift was. "Whoever it is, they can wait. Everyone who matters is here so it can't be that important, right?"

"What if it's Council business? You are the Regulator, after all." Aidan seemed all too eager for me to answer my phone which made me even more suspicious. Did he know what my present was? I was getting the impression it was something bigger than the Shamrock Fest concert tickets I asked for.

The ringtone, which happened to be set to Bad Religion's version of Father Christmas, meant it wasn't a number in my contacts. I liked to assign ringtones so I knew who called without needing to actually look at the phone. If Agrona was calling, my phone would play the Wicked Witch theme song from *Wizard of Oz*, so I knew it wasn't her. Before I could explain that to everyone so we could get back to the giving and receiving of gifts and I could find out what Mason was up to, my phone gave us yet another lesson about the materialistic nature of the holidays in the form of a catchy punk tune.

Still not adjusted to her sensitive vampiric hearing, Ryanne jumped from her seat, raced into the kitchen, snatched my phone off the counter and tossed it across the apartment. Dre threw a hand out and caught my phone before it connected with my face.

"Sorry, if you don't mind getting that." Ryanne sat

back down and delicately crossed her legs, her hands resting on her knee.

"I was kind of in the middle of something here." Mason didn't hide his disappointment at the interruption but waved me on. "Go ahead, get it. Whoever it is isn't going to stop."

"Kincaide here." Not the most professional greeting but it worked for me.

"Maurin, it's Mike over at the bar. Sorry to call on your personal cell like this but we've got trouble."

I skipped the bad joke about trouble literally being in the name of the bar. "I wouldn't have given you the number if I never expected you to call. However, I'm kind of in the middle of a solstice party right now and since I'm the hostess I can't really leave. Why are you laughing? Do you have a problem or not?"

"Sorry, it's just I never pictured you as a hostess. And yes, we have a problem here."

"I'll have you know I make an apron look damn good. Anyway, as I was saying, I can't come down right now but the Council's got a small team on call for nights I'm off. I can have Amalie put a call in to Agrona now if you want."

"Amalie's there? Good, that will save me a call. Bring her with you."

"Mike, did you even hear what I said? I can't come down there."

"This isn't like a rowdy group of college kids on Black Out Wednesday or some drunk who can't handle their Solstice shooters. There's something weird about these witches, Maurin. Their magic feels dirty. They've run off most of my regulars. I don't want some half ass crew coming in here and busting my bar all to hell. I'm asking you to do it. Or do I need to remind you of the outstanding bar tab you and your friends ran up last weekend."

"Hey, you said that was on the house since we tossed those two fang bangers and their pimp out of the bar for you. We came in to have a quick drink after closing a case. You didn't even know they were setting up shop selling nips and sips by the pool tables." I couldn't believe Mike was trying to drop that bill on me. I drank a lot of damn vodka I wouldn't have if I'd known I was paying for it. Aidan was our designated driver but the rest of our team drank their weight in booze and blood. It would take a week's wages to pay the bill and Mike's prices weren't that high.

"Well, I never asked you to throw them out and I never put in a formal request for a cleaner so far as I can tell, you owe for the bill. Now, you can come down here and settle up. I'll take it in cash or services. It's up to you."

"Someone is going to put in a formal request for a cleaner for you if I come down there tonight, Mike. I can't believe you're pulling this shit."

"Maurin, what are we arguing about here? You're the Regulator. It's your job. And I'm telling you right now, if those newbies show up instead of you, the Council's on the hook for the damages and you're on the hook for the tab." Mike hung up.

Typically, when a cleaning crew goes in the hiring party is responsible for any damages. When the Council is the hiring party, our fees and any damages are paid out of the seized funds from the guilty party. I knew Mike would pay for damages regardless of the newbie team. There was no way the Council would agree because then everyone else would want damages covered and there goes the profit margin. Still, the hassle of dealing with Mike and the Council while they argued wasn't worth it because then I'd have to send a message to pay and find another bar to drink at.

And I really liked Toil and Trouble.

I looked at my father, then at Mason silently asking their approval to go. The party had been more for the two of them than anyone else and I didn't want to ruin it, although I was pretty sure Mike already had. The rest of the evening would be tainted, a cloud hanging over us raining *what ifs* all over the party.

"I'm coming with you." Mason looked a bit broken-hearted that Mike ruined his big moment and I wondered again exactly what his gift for me was. "Go get changed."

Torn between the first holiday happiness I'd ever experienced and the rush of the chase, I gave him a quick kiss and headed for my bedroom. I swapped my black leggings and black cotton skirt for a pair of jeans but kept the Grinch tee, slipping on my oxblood eight hole Docs and pulling on my knitted cap with the skull on it and my leather jacket. A lot less layers than when I went shopping but I could not kick ass if I looked like the Staypuft Marshmallow Man.

"You're going to freeze." Mason wrapped a scarf around my neck and tucked it into my coat. "Let's go. Aidan's already warming up the car."

"We'll meet you there." Cash stood up, Nolak beside him.

"There's no sense in ruining everyone's night. Stay here with Arawn and Ryanne. It's just a few witches who had too much to drink, popping spells at Mike and the customers. We'll be in and out." I tugged my knit hat over my ears.

"Mike wouldn't have called you on your cell if it was that easy." Cash zipped up his coat. Wolves ran hotter than the rest of us, something to do with their metabolism, but their skin would still be exposed to the elements so contrary to popular belief werewolves did not run around half naked all the time. Especially not in the winter.

"Just stay, we can handle it. We'll be back before you know it. Tonight was going great, like perfect. If you leave then my father probably will and then Ryanne will be alone in my apartment. Seriously, stay."

Cash smirked, knowing that the idea of Ryanne alone at my place would have me worried the entire time that she'd be rooting through my stuff. She'd given no signs of being a snoop, quite the opposite in fact, since she was Mason's trusted housekeeper in Ireland before being turned by Aidan. Still, you couldn't be too careful.

"So you'll wait?" I asked, before whistling for Conry.

"If you're not back by…" Cash looked at his watch. "Eleven, we're coming after you." He glanced at Nolak, who nodded his agreement.

That gave us two hours to get there, bust up the band of rowdy witches, and get back. Piece of cake. We'd be back well before midnight and the official moment of Solstice.

We piled, or rather squeezed, into the Camaro. Amalie rode shotgun while I sat in the back sandwiched between Mason and Conry. It took less than fifteen minutes to get to the bar.

Abandoned by his regulars and even a couple staff members, Mike stood alone behind the counter. A few broken liquor bottles dripped their contents onto the shelves beneath them behind him. The jukebox's neon lights flickered, highlighting the broken glass around it. I'd played Joan Jett's *Bad Reputation* more times than I could count on that thing. It would be a shame to see it replaced with satellite radio.

A cue ball rolled across the floor from the busted pool table in the back, breaking the heavy silence which hung in the air. He wasn't kidding when he called. The place was trashed.

"Where's Josh and Malcolm?" I asked, concerned that the two guys who normally bounced for him weren't stationed at the door or anywhere in sight.

"They're gone." His eyes quickly shifted to his feet and back up, letting me know *gone* meant dead.

"You said you had some trouble with a couple patrons tonight?" I scanned the bar, my friends fanning out behind me but I couldn't sense anyone else inside. "You manage to run them off on your own?" I knew he hadn't. My skin crawled from the dark energy swirling around us.

"It's a cloaking spell." Amalie whispered in my ear, seconds before a blast of magic was fired in our direction.

I shoved her down and dove to my right, flipping a table and two chairs, bruising my hip on the way down. Acid ate through the floor next to Amalie. They'd tried to hit me, not her. I couldn't say I was entirely surprised since I was responsible for the trial and conviction of Salem's High Priestess. Mahalia tried to murder me but that point seemed irrelevant to most of the witches left behind. I used the table as a shield, peering over the top to get a look at our attackers.

The cloaking spell lost its usefulness the moment they fired their first shot. Four witches stood before us, one of them holding a hostage. I'd seen the girl in here before, usually after she finished a shift at the Stop 'n' Shop. Just a townie out for a drink, caught up in a shit storm.

The witch held onto her despite her struggles to break free, one hand crushing her throat. She stopped fighting when he pressed his pointer finger to her temple, his hand in the shape of a gun. Her eyes grew wide with fear, tears slipping down her cheeks. With that kind of reaction, she'd seen him do this to someone else and knew the gesture wasn't just pretend. I figured there were more than two bodies lying behind that bar with Mike.

Amalie fired a blast of her own magic back. Since taking my place as liaison, she hadn't been in the line of fire but she showed no signs of rust. Amalie hit the hostage in the chest, knocking her back and out of the arms of the black witch before he fired his shot. The girl dropped to the ground, scurrying away as the misfire of dark magic hit the long mirror behind Mike, raining shards of glass everywhere.

Mike ducked down behind the counter, shouting profanities and promises that they were going to pay for this. I still wasn't sure who they were, these witches didn't look local, but Mike was right. They were going to pay.

The poor girl from the grocery store didn't make it very far. Another witch snatched her hair, pulling her up off the floor. The girl didn't struggle, she simply hung limp from the witch's hands as the life was sucked out of her. Renewed power and strength radiated from the witch as she tossed the withered husk of a girl on the floor.

Magic exploded.

Frigid air rushed in through the blown out windows and doors. Amalie stood in the center of her circle of protection. She'd set it fast and wide enough to protect us all. Black orbs, curses meant to kill, exploded harmlessly around us. Safe for the moment, but no closer to stopping the dark witches.

"You can't stay in that circle forever, Regulator. We've got all night. Your little witch will tire eventually, one of the dark witches called out.

So they knew who I was. They came for me. Wasn't the first time, wouldn't be the last.

"He's right. We can't stay in here forever." Dre opened and closed his fists, obviously itching to be released from the protective bubble.

"Four witches, powerful witches, using blood magic. If I drop this shield they'll hit us with death curses. I don't think I can stop them all." The sparkle left Amalie's eyes, the fear I felt that we might not make it out alive mirrored in her gaze.

"Then it's a good thing I'm mostly dead already." Dre broke through the circle, charging forward when the mini-blood coven expected us to cower.

From there, chaos ruled. Magic exploded in all directions as Amalie countered their attack. Aidan and Dre moved lightning fast, catching one of the witches from behind. I'd never seen someone drawn and quartered before. I could do without seeing it again. The torso fell to the floor, each vampire tossing limbs as they rushed for the next.

A second later, two stakes flew through the air. Dre took one in the chest, dropping instantly. Aidan tried to block the one aimed for him, the sharpened Rowan wood going through his hand, pinning it to his chest. Still, he rushed forward, slashing out with his good hand. He struck the witch hard, shredding flesh and knocking her back to Conry so my guardian could finish the job.

Two down and two to go.

Mason and I ran toward the dark witches, dodging black curses and being peppered with lead buckshot. I took a hit in the left shoulder. Mason took one in the ribs but we pressed forward. Daggers drawn I dropped, sliding across a floor I would have preferred never to come in contact with and slicing the Achilles tendon of the witch closest to me. Mason caught him as his leg gave out, snapping his neck on the way down.

Amalie threw out a spell, slamming it into the last witch. Apparently satisfied with the results of her magic, she toed the unconscious dark witch. "Hmm, it worked."

"You weren't sure?" Dre muttered from the floor, rubbing the spot where Aidan pulled the stake out of his chest. Half an inch more and he wouldn't have been able to say anything at all.

"It's a binding spell out of the book Maurin gave me. You can't always tell with the older grimmoires, a lot of them are fakes, but I figured it was worth a shot." Amalie pulled out her cell to call Agrona. If a blood coven came to take me out and look for new recruits, the Council needed to be notified.

"What's that mark? There on his wrist, some sort of tattoo?" I pulled the witch's sleeve up to get a better look at the design.

"It's not a tattoo. It's drawn on the skin, some sort of black grease paint." Mason pulled out his phone and took a picture of the pattern which went further up the dead man's forearm than I'd originally thought.

"Some sort of warding?" I took a picture with my own phone. The more documentation, the better.

"None I've ever seen." Apparently as baffled by the symbols as the rest of us, Amalie leaned in for a closer look. "I've never seen anything like these."

Mason gently moved Amalie's hand away. "Don't touch."

"Why, do you think it's a curse?" Amalie pulled her hand back.

"I'm not sure but I don't think we should touch it." Mason thought for a moment. "Can you loosen the binding spell? Enough to ask him a few questions but not enough he can go back to slinging curses at us?"

"The only way to truly stop a witch from spelling is to cut out their tongue, eyes, and cut off their hands." Amalie frowned. "I don't know if I should tweak the spell."

The witch on the floor seized, spittle landing on the corner of his chin. We watched him die, unable to stop it.

He wasn't talking to anyone. Ever again.

Nothing left to do but wait for the crew on call to come and clean up. The same crew I tried to send when Mike called in the first place. They'd set the place right, wipe it clean, and then we'd all be on the trail of the blood coven moving into Salem. We knew there were more than four and we planned on finding them.

I left Mike bitching about the state of the bar, reminding him he'd insisted I come down and clear out the dark witches. Job done. Payment for damages and the crew would come from the dead witches' accounts. Just as soon as we found out who they were. More motivation for the second string coming in behind us to work faster and harder.

Mason followed me outside with my knit hat and scarf in his hands. "You're going to freeze."

"It's not any warmer in there." I leaned in when he wrapped my scarf around my neck, stealing a quick kiss.

He pulled the small bough of mistletoe from inside his coat pocket, not one berry or leaf crushed. How had he managed to keep it safe during the meltdown inside Toil and Trouble? Luck or a little solstice magic? Probably both.

I didn't wait for him to hold it up above our heads.

Cradling his face with both hands, I drew him in. Our lips touched, gently at first, until the lingering adrenaline from the fight inside ignited our passion for one another. His hand slid along my back pressing me against him, moving lower, easing inside my back jeans pocket.

With one hand fisted in his hair, I slid the other up his shirt, tracing my fingertips along each perfectly defined muscle. In a flurry of hands and lips, he backed me against the wall, the icy bricks acting like a cold shower.

With a sigh, he dropped his head on my shoulder. "Back to your place?"

"We won't be finishing this there, either. The Solstice party, remember?"

"We could go back to my place. We still have about an hour before Cash sends the pack out."

I rested my head against the bricks, weighing my options while a crowd formed outside the bar. "We should go back. They'll be worried."

He kissed me again, this one shorter than the last but missing none of the passion. "You're right. They'll be worried." Another kiss. "We should get back."

"The sooner we get back, the sooner the party will be over. The sooner everyone will go home." I managed to get out between more kisses. "And I never got to give you your gift."

"Which reminds me. I never got to give you yours."

Mason reached in to his inner coat pocket and pulled out a small turquoise box wrapped with a white ribbon. My heart stammered in my chest.

It was a Tiffany's box. Even I recognized that. I also knew the box was too small for a necklace or a watch. Earrings? I prayed the beautiful blue box held a pair of extravagant earrings I'd never wear and insist he take back.

I wasn't ready for anything more and I couldn't bear the thought of losing him because we were at different places in our lives. I'd get there eventually and staring at that little jewelry box in his hand I realized I wanted to get there with him. But I knew it was too soon.

Some of the people who came out to see what happened to Mike's bar noticed the box in Mason's hand. So did our friends when they stepped outside looking for us. A small crowd gathered with eager faces, waiting for my boyfriend to get on one knee and ask me that magical question and make me his fiancé.

Everyone except Aidan. He didn't quite have a scowl on his face but it certainly wasn't joy either. I bit back the fear of saying *no* in front of all those people or taking the ring and saying *no* later when we were alone as I waited for him to kneel down.

But he never did. He just opened the box, the tiny hinges creaking a little. I felt sick. The words *don't throw up, don't throw up*, played over and over in my mind. Panicked, I feared that's how I would end up answering his question.

When the outside spotlight finally hit the inside of the box, a sterling silver ring glimmered at me. A ring too big to fit on my finger. A small silver tag with the Tiffany and Co. logo engraved on one side and a date engraved on the other.

"It goes with this." Mason held up an ordinary door key.

A key ring. The man bought me a key ring from Tiffany's. Relief and, to my surprise, a little disappointment flooded me. The crowd dispersed, disappointed they weren't a part of what should be a private moment.

I took the key, turning it in my hand. One day he'd give me a box with an engagement ring inside. One day I'd say yes. The fact he knew this wasn't the day made me love him even more.

I smiled at him. "I think we should go to your

place."

"What about the Solstice party?" Mason's eyes were alight with mischief.

"I want to try out my gift. Besides, we've got almost an hour, remember." I whispered promises to show him why I made the naughty list and walked off in the direction of his apartment. This was one solstice neither of us would forget.

Dear Reader,

I hope you enjoyed reading *Mistletoe Meltdown*. I love hearing from readers. Your feedback is extremely important to me, so please leave a review on the site where you purchased this book.

Want to know more about new releases, events, contests and giveaways? Be sure to check out my Facebook page www.facebook.com/TheMaurinKincaideSeries. It's a great way to keep in touch and I try to interact as often as I can on the page.

Thank you so much for your continued support.

Rachel Rawlings

www.rachelrawlings.com
twitter: @rachelsbooks
www.facebook.com/TheMaurinKincaideSeries
www.tsu.com/rachelsbooks
www.hallowread.com
www.facebook.com/hallowread

www.ingramcontent.com/pod-product-compliance
Lightning Source LLC
Chambersburg PA
CBHW070653130626
46555CB00006B/2858